For Kason, my favorite little monkey.

Manny the Monkey was written with the intentions of guiding Children to search for what they want to do in life, in a fun and unique way through the eye of a traveling Monkey. Madison, who has always had a passion for traveling and animals decided to combine the two loves of her life and turn it into a fun and playful story! Born and raised in California, exiting her college career, Madison found a hard time finding her life purpose and along the way has found her path in writing thanks to the support of family and friends, inspiring the story of *Manny the Monkey*. She, now through the story of Manny, hopes to ignite the flame in others that it is okay to be lost because you will find yourself along the way!

© Madison Mooney 2019

ISBN: 978-1-54396-271-0

Manny
THE
MONKEY

BY MADISON MOONEY

Manny the Monkey is smart and he is funny.
Now he has to find something to do to make money.
Manny likes this but he also likes that.
The little monkey just wants to find something he is good at.

And just like that, he got a thought in his head.
To travel the animal kingdom and see what options lie ahead.
Manny started packing his things, excited to listen and learn.
Adventure was calling, for it was his turn!

Manny decided to talk to his Mom and Dad
To listen to all the advice that they had.

"Mama and Papa, it is time for me to go.
I must travel the world so that I can grow!
I am a little monkey but please do not be scared
Do you have any advice that will leave me prepared?"

"We are monkeys. We are both creative and smart.
We believe in you little Monkey, with our whole hearts!
This journey will be tough but also insightful.
No matter what, remember that every part of you is delightful!"

"I am not as smart as you, Papa. Nor am I as creative as you.
So what must a little monkey like myself do!?
I must travel the world and that is a fact.
Until I find something I am really good at!"

With that being said, Manny the monkey grabbed his bag and walked outside
It was the push that he needed to follow the direction of the tide.
He jumped in a ship and started to set sail
That is when Manny bumped into a whale!

"Hi. Mr. Whale, I am traveling the world to find something I am good at.
Do you mind telling me what you do to help get me up to bat?"

"I am a Blue Whale. I am the largest animal of them all.
I like to shoot water out of my blowhole over 30 feet tall!
When it comes to being big, I am the best!
Do you do anything better than the rest?"

"I am not that big and I am not that large.
But I must say I am pretty good at taking charge.
Again I must go to travel some more

Until I find exactly what I am looking for!"

Manny sailed away until he saw a fish near the top of the water.
It was a clown fish, right there in the saltwater!
He stopped the boat as fast as he could
And asked the fish what he thought he should.

"Hi Mr. Clown Fish, how are you?
Do you have some time to tell me what you do?"

"I am a Fish and I am a Clown.
I have always been keen on messing around.
I make people laugh, that is what I do.
Is this something you are good at too?"

"I can tell a good joke when I am near a friend
I make my friends laugh but that is something I do on the weekend
If I make people laugh, I will have a good time
But I don't think I would make more than a dime!"

Manny thanked the clown fish and went on his way
He decided to leave the ocean and fly without delay!
The first thing he did was book a flight
He booked the first flight out to Africa that night!

As soon as he landed, he booked a Safari ride
And to his amazement the first thing he saw was a Lion's pride!
He was so excited that he opened his door.
Then the king of the pride let out his roar.

"I am sorry to have startled you Mr. Lion but I had a quick question.
Do you mind telling me about your profession?"

"I am a Lion, I am very proud.
I am very strong and I can roar real loud.
I rule my lands and watch over my pride.
Is courage something that you can provide?"

"When it comes to courage, I am not the best.
I must say though, I am really good at beating on my chest!
I am not the strongest but I can be loud
If I stand up for something, my family would be proud!"

Manny liked what the lion had to say
But during the discussion he heard someone neigh
He looked to his left and saw a zebra across the grassland.
Where Manny wanted to talk about his trade in hand.

"Hello Mr. Zebra, I noticed you from across the way.
Do you have any talents that might help me at the end of the day?"

"I am a Zebra. I am both black and white.
My colors help me defend myself in a fight.
I am very fast, with a powerful kick
Were you born with cool colors or a really cool trick?"

"I am not very fast and I do not like to fight
But I guess I am known for being very bright
When it comes to a kick, I would need help from a friend
However, my smarts may help me out in the end!"

Manny thought that the Zebra was very smart
But knew it was time for him to depart
At that moment, he heard a loud sound
It came from an elephant whose foot had just touched the ground.

"Why hello there Mr. Elephant, my name is Manny the monkey
Do you have any talents that are pretty funky?"

"I am an Elephant. I am known for my excellent
memory and my big ears.
I can travel for miles and my tusks help to
protect me from all of my fears.
I enjoy showing off my emotions and tend to
use my whole body to communicate.
Do you think your memory is where your
future will await?"

"I am very good at remembering things that touch my heart!
Like you, I use my emotions to help guide me from the start.
I may not be the best at using my mind
But maybe my personality will help with what I need to find."

Manny thanked Mr. Elephant for all of his time
But when he walked away he stepped in some slime
He looked down at his foot and saw the gross water
And that is when the crocodile came out from underwater.

"Hey there! Mr. Crocodile, you came out of nowhere!
Do you do anything cool that you would like to share?"

"I am a Crocodile. I have a very strong bite.
I am excellent at swimming and I am very good at keeping out of sight!
I am very patient and not afraid to snap at anything that comes along!
Are you good at hunting or are you not very strong?"

"I do not like to swim, unless it is a hot day
Although, I am very patient especially when things are not going my way.
I may not be good at staying strong
But I have been patient all along!"

The Crocodile was a bit tired, so Manny went on his way
When he saw something tall and spotted right behind a stack of hay
He looked at the animal and could not help but notice its long neck
Manny didn't know if he should talk to him but then thought, "Oh, what the heck"!

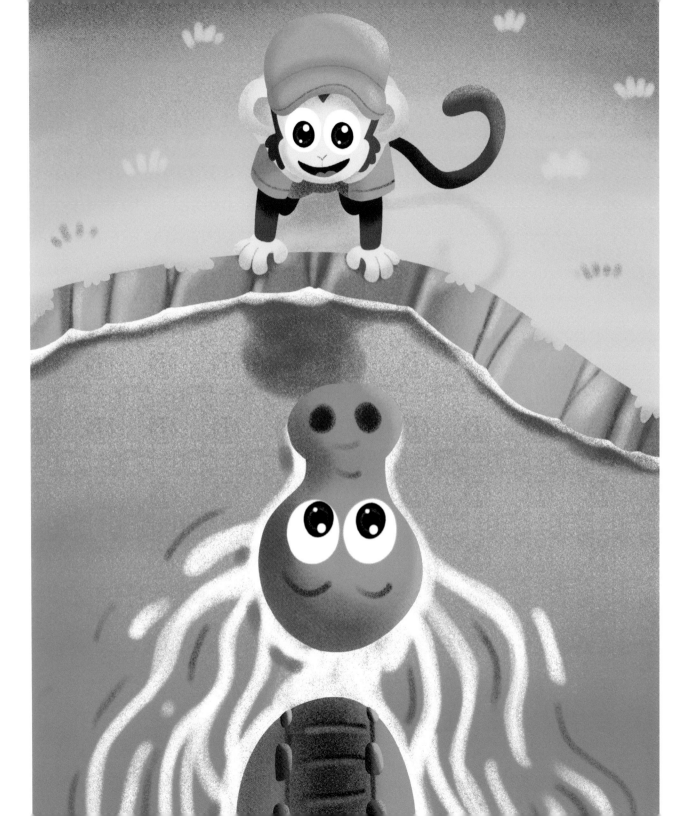

"Hello Mr. Giraffe", Manny shouted, "I have something to ask.
Do you do anything neat or have a cool task?"

"I am a Giraffe. I am very tall.
My vision and height help me protect
my family and prey that are too small.
I am calm and steady and am ready to
defend.
Is your eyesight something that would
help you bend to bend?"

"I am not very tall and I can't see that far
But I would protect my family even if it would leave me with a scar
I guess I am not the tallest in height but maybe I am at heart
Thank you for helping me realize that I have defended my family
from the start!"

It was at that moment that Manny the monkey came to realize
All of the other animals helped him believe that he was, oh so wise.
Manny had what he needed inside him all along
Now it was time to go home and voice his inner song!

"I am not like a Zebra nor am I whale
I am not like anyone, I need to make my own trail
I may not know exactly what I am going to do
What are your thoughts on my breakthrough?"

"Momma and Papa, I have returned back home
I learned something very important, meaning I am my own.
I should not compare myself to another
With this journey, I had my own self to discover."

"You are smart and you are kind.
You can do anything as long as you use your mind.
You are unique and you are one.
Just be who you are and always have fun!"

"Thank you Mama and Papa for telling me what is true!
I am an amazing little monkey and I cannot wait to see what I can and will do!"